FLOOD

"Todd climbed to the second floor, where the flat was, and found the things that Mum wanted.

But how was he going to get to North London?

Then he heard a voice in the hall. Someone had seen him.

'Marston! You're dead!'"

D0453254

FLOOD

Fifteen great
SHARP SHADES 2.0 *reads:*

SHARP SHADES 2.0

FLOOD

David Orme

Ransom

SHARP SHADES 2.0
Flood
by David Orme

Published by Ransom Publishing Ltd.
Unit 7, Brocklands Farm, West Meon, Hampshire GU32 1JN, UK
www.ransom.co.uk

ISBN   978 178127 980 9
First published in 2016

Copyright © 2016 Ransom Publishing Ltd.
Text copyright © 2016 David Orme
Cover photograph copyright © jcrosemann. Other images copyright © davidf; Tony
Baggett; EHStock; davedesignmethod; paolofur; chrisdorney; Herianus; thelinke;
Reddiplomat; Peter Zelei.

A CIP catalogue record of this book is available from the British Library.

All rights reserved. No part of this publication may be reproduced, stored in a
retrieval system, or transmitted, in any form or by any means, electronic, mechanical,
photocopying, recording or otherwise, without the prior permission of the publishers.

The right of David Orme to be identified as the author of this Work has been
asserted by him in accordance with sections 77 and 78 of the Copyright, Design and
Patents Act 1988.

CONTENTS

INTRODUCTION

The summer of 2025 had been hot, but the winter was wet. There were floods across the country. Roads were blocked and railway lines had been washed away.

The weather had been like this for ten years. The climate was changing. The world was getting hotter, and the weather more violent.

By February, the Thames Valley was under threat. Whole towns had been flooded. The great swollen river, trapped between concrete banks, swept eastwards towards the sea. But first it had to pass through London.

So far the embankments had stopped most of the flooding, though in some places the drains had overflowed. Houses had been filled with stinking sewage.

There was worse to come. February the fourteenth was the make or break day.

The Thames Barrier had protected London for fifty years. It was being used more and more often, especially at the spring tides. These happened once a month. At these times the tides were highest. A huge new barrier was being built, but this wouldn't be ready for another five years.

February the fourteenth was the next spring tide. Usually, the barrier would do its job, but there was a problem. If the barrier was lifted, the great flood of river water would start backing up. And this water was dangerously high already.

The experts thought everything would be all right.

'It will be close, but we don't expect serious flooding,' they said.

People began to relax. It looked as if London would be safe.

But by February the thirteenth, weather reports were coming in, and things began to look very bad.

ONE

Southwark Crown Court, London
February 14th, 11 am

'How do you find the defendant?
Guilty, or not guilty?'
    'Guilty.'
    There was shouting in the court.
    'We'll get you, Marston!' someone

yelled.

The troublemakers were taken out. They were from the prisoner's family. In the witness room, Todd Marston heard the noise. He guessed what they were saying.

Todd had given evidence against Mickey Turner. His friends had told him not to. They said that the Turners would come for him.

Todd wouldn't listen. Mickey Turner sold drugs. The drugs sometimes had dangerous chemicals mixed in them. Todd's best friend had died after taking them.

Todd didn't care about the risk.

He wanted to see Mickey punished.

In the court, the judge was about to pass sentence. Before he could speak, sirens started to howl outside. The judge was given a note.

'Please could everyone leave the building,' he said. 'There is a serious risk of flooding from the river.' He turned to the prisoner. 'You will be sentenced later.'

Todd wondered what was going on. He opened the door and looked out. A policeman was moving people out of the building.

'What's going on?'

'Flood warning. Get out as quickly as you can.'

'I can't go yet. I'm in danger from the Turners. Someone said they would take me to the safe house where my mother is.'

'I'll see what I can do, but there's an emergency.'

Todd saw some of the Turner family. He went back into the witness room quickly.

A few minutes later, he looked out again. The policeman was checking that everyone had gone.

'Come on, leave the building now!'

'I can't! The Turners'll be waiting for me! I was a witness in the trial!'

'Come with me. You can leave through the jury entrance and slip away. Contact the police when the flooding is over. I'm sorry; it's all I can do.'

The jury entrance was near the river. The water was almost up to the top of the wall.

There was a cold wind. Todd pulled up the hood of his anorak. With his face hidden, the Turners might not find him. People who grassed on them usually ended up dead.

TWO

Met Office Headquarters, Exeter, Devon
February 14th, 12 Noon

A group of weathermen were in a video-conference with the Prime Minister.

'So, we are heading for a major disaster?'

'Yes, Prime Minister. Our guess is that by eight o'clock tonight a good part of Central London will be under water, especially south of the river. There's going to be a lot of damage. People need to be evacuated *now*.'

'But up to a few days ago you said that there was no danger! What has happened?'

'We have been tracking an area of deep depression for some days. We thought we had worked out its track, but we got it wrong. Yesterday afternoon it changed direction and moved down the North Sea. This made a storm surge.

With the Spring tides, the sea was about three metres higher than usual.

'The surge is heading for the

Channel. That's where the water gets squeezed into the mouth of the Thames. The winds are coming from the east, pushing huge waves into the estuary. Everything has come together at the same time – the storm, the spring tide and the floods.'

'What about the Thames Barrier?'

'It can't keep this amount of water back, especially with the floodwater coming down the river. There's nothing we can do.'

THREE

Southwark, London
February 14th, 12 Noon

Todd switched on his mobile. He had
to tell Mum what was happening.
Mum was in their new flat in North
London. The police had moved
them there before the trial.

Todd hoped the Turners would never find them there.

'Hi, Mum. It's over. Guilty. Look, Mum, the police are tied up because of the flood scare. I'll have to make my own way to the flat.'

'What about my stuff from the old flat?'

Todd had forgotten that. The police were going to take him there on the way to the new flat. The old flat was the last place he wanted to go to.

'Todd, I really need those things.'

Todd sighed.

'OK, Mum. I've got the list. See you later.'

The water was trickling over the stone wall next to the river. Suddenly there was a crashing sound. One of the stone blocks had been pushed out. A great waterfall poured through the gap.

Todd had to get away from there. He turned down Battle Bridge into Tooley Street.

Everything was chaos. The road was clogged with cars and vans. All the time, the sirens were wailing.

Todd walked quickly to the tube station, but when he got there the station was closed. He would have to walk.

As he plodded down the Borough Road, he noticed something strange. Water was gushing *up* through the drains and spreading out across the road.

The traffic splashed through the water, sending waves over the pavement. Todd was soon soaked.

At last, he reached the old flat. It was in a block. He had never liked living there. Some people were busy moving out. Even flats weren't good places to be when there were floods. The toilets wouldn't work, and there would be no electricity or gas. But many of the people there were old, and would be staying. They had nowhere else to go.

Todd climbed to the second floor, where the flat was, and found the things that Mum wanted.

But how was he going to get to North London?

Then he heard a voice in the hall. Someone had seen him.

'Marston! You're dead!'

FOUR

White Hart Estate, Lambeth,
London
February 14th, 3 pm

Todd had been sure that they were
going to kill him, then and there.
But they didn't.

'Move.'

'Where are you taking me?'

'Don't talk, just move.'

The three men marched Todd out of the flat and down the stairs. There were still a few people about. They turned away at the sight of Todd and the ugly-looking toughs.

Not my business, they thought. *I've got other things to worry about.*

Todd guessed he was going to be pushed into a car. He had worked out their plan: *don't murder him here; everyone would know who had done it. Do him in somewhere nice and quiet, where no one could hear him screaming.*

But they didn't leave the building

at the ground floor. They carried on down to boiler room in the basement.

They opened the door and pushed Todd inside. Todd's arms were forced behind his back and tied up with wire. Then he was pushed to the ground and more wire was tied round his ankles. Finally, brown tape was wound round his mouth.

One of the gang gave him a vicious kick in the back.

'That's the last time you grass up the Turners, Marston,' he said.

The three men left the underground room. Todd heard the

door slam and the key turn in the lock.

Todd looked around. There was a row of boilers, switched off because of the emergency, and one window just under the ceiling, letting in a little grey light.

He had thought the Turners were going to kill him. So why was he still alive?

Suddenly the light went out, and the window shattered in an explosion of water and glass.

FIVE

The Newsroom, New Broadcasting House, London
February 14th, 3.30 pm

In the newsroom everything was chaos. Reporters were sending in reports from all over London, and live pictures were beaming in from helicopters and CCTV. They

showed people hanging out of high windows waiting to be rescued, or even sitting on rooftops.

The emergency services were finding it difficult to cope, and there were still four and a half hours to go before high tide.

The east wind was still fierce and the storm surge was still very high in the English Channel.

Floodwater was still backing up all along the river. It would probably be days, even weeks, before the floods finally went.

The newsreader was reading out government advice.

'Move to family or friends on higher ground. But if the roads are flooded, do not leave your home. Wait for rescue. If you know of elderly or sick people in flooded areas, let the emergency services know. Do not drink water from the tap. Turn off the gas and electricity. Only use your mobile phones for essential calls. Try and keep warm by wearing extra clothes ... '

Suddenly, the studio lights went out. Just as suddenly, they came back on, as back-up generators started. The newsreader looked at a note he had been given.

'Electricity supplies in the London

area are to be switched off', he announced. 'Telephone services, including mobile services, are breaking down across the whole of southern England. We are sorry to say that all television services will be closing down at four o'clock today.'

The news report cut to a picture of two important-looking people standing on a platform.

'Earlier today the Prime Minister and the Mayor of London spoke to the people of London. They told everyone to remain calm ... '

All across London, people who still had electricity were switching off their television sets. As if the floods weren't bad enough, without having to listen to those two.

SIX

White Hart Estate, Lambeth, London
February 14th, 3.45 pm

The underground room was quickly filling up with water. If Todd didn't do something fast, he would drown.

He managed to wriggle to the wall. Twisting round, he started to push with his legs. Slowly, he managed to push himself upright.

The water was already up to his knees. Once the room was full of water, there was no chance.

Now he realised what the Turners had planned. Why bother to murder him when the river would do it for them?

There was almost no light to see by. Todd looked down at the rising water. It was coming in under the door as well as through the window. It was freezing cold and stinking.

He guessed he had maybe ten minutes before the room was flooded to the ceiling. With the tape around his mouth, he couldn't even call for help.

The freezing water crept higher and higher. Todd was shaking, and it wasn't just the cold. He didn't want to die. He didn't want to leave his mum. How would she manage without him?

The water was now nearly up to his neck, and the smell was terrible. Todd glanced up at the window. Then he looked again. The water had stopped pouring in! Maybe it wouldn't get any higher.

Half an hour passed. He didn't think he could stand it much longer. He had to get out of there.

He had been working at the tape round his mouth, pushing at it with his tongue. At last he felt it moving. He could open his mouth, at least partly.

'Help!'

No answer.

Of course there wouldn't be. No one would hear him down there. Todd yelled again and again, on and on, though he was sure it was hopeless.

And then, at last, he heard the

voice of an old woman.

'Who's there? Are you all right?'

Yes of course I'm all right, thought Todd. *That's why I'm standing here up to my neck in sewage, screaming my head off.*

SEVEN

Fire and Rescue Service Call Centre, Southwark Bridge Road, London
February 14th, 4.20 – 5 pm

'What's that you say? Someone trapped in a basement? Where? Elm House, White Hart Estate. And your name? Mrs Andrews. Thank you for calling. We'll be

there as soon as we can.'

Every fire engine was out on the roads. A call about someone trapped in a basement was urgent, but the fire brigade had been dealing with calls like that all day.

Within a quarter of an hour, the rescue team had reached the block of flats. The leading fireman called back on his radio.

'It's a young lad. Trapped in the boiler room. Says he's been tied up so he can't get out. There's about five feet of sewage in there.'

The firemen managed to smash

the lock, but the door wouldn't open because of the weight of water on both sides.

In the end, they smashed the door to pieces and managed to haul Todd out. He was shivering and exhausted.

'Whoever did this to you? You need to get to hospital, lad, but it's not going to be easy. Where do you live?'

'Flat 12, second floor.'

'Have you got something you can change into there?'

Luckily there were still some of Todd's clothes in his wardrobe at the flat.

'Right. Go and get some warm clothes on. We'll call an ambulance, but I'm afraid it's going to take them some time to get here. OK?'

Todd nodded. His teeth were chattering and it was hard to talk.

He staggered up the stairs to the flat. It was almost completely dark now. Luckily, Todd knew his way round.

He managed to strip off his clothes and clean himself as best he could with cold water and towels. Then he put on clean clothes. He had tried ringing his mother, but the network was down.

He knew he couldn't wait. What if the Turners came back?

He took an old coat from the wardrobe and put it on. Then he left the flat and set off towards the river.

Behind him, someone stepped out of a doorway and began to follow him.

EIGHT

Lambeth, London
February 14th, 6.30 – 7.30 pm

Todd had never known London so dark. If he hadn't known the area all his life, he would soon have got lost.

He headed for the nearest bridge,

but ahead he saw flashing blue lights. A police car. Two policemen were standing there.

'You can't go this way, pal. Water's too deep. Where are you trying to get to?'

'I've got to get across the river. It's urgent!'

'I'd go home if I were you, and stay away from the river.'

'But I live the other side of the river! I've got to get back to my mum!'

The other policeman joined in. 'The last time I heard, Westminster Bridge was still open. You could try that. But I'd wait till the morning, when the water's gone down a bit.'

'Thanks, I'll do that.'

But Todd wasn't going to do that. Westminster Bridge wasn't far. He would try there.

At last, Todd reached Westminster Bridge Road and turned towards the river. Almost straight away he was into water.

He couldn't give up now. He started to wade through it.

Immediately he was grabbed from behind. He felt a knife at his throat.

'Got you!'

Todd knew that voice.
It was Mickey Turner.

NINE

Westminster Bridge, London
February 14th, 8 pm

Somehow, Mickey had managed to escape from the court. He probably meant to leave the country. But he had someone to deal with first. Todd.

Mickey was evil and savage, but he wasn't stupid. If anyone was looking out of a window, they would see what was going on. He began to drag Todd towards the buildings at the side of the road.

Suddenly, Todd felt Mickey lose his grip. He began to fall. Todd almost fell as well. He stepped back to steady himself and felt the edge of a hole beneath his feet. An open manhole! Mickey had stepped backwards, straight into it.

Quickly Todd was off, heading towards the bridge. He hoped that Mickey would fall right down the hole, but he had managed to stop himself going completely down. He was able to pull himself out. He started after Todd, shouting threats.

When Todd reached the bridge, the water was above his waist. He knew that Mickey was bigger and stronger than he was. He could hold Todd under water and wait until he drowned. No one would ever know it was murder.

The bridge rose higher towards the middle. By the time Todd was half-way across, the water was only a few inches deep. He started to run towards the Westminster side.

Ahead of him, by the Houses of Parliament, he saw a bus, but only the top deck. The rest was under water.

There was no escape. The water was too deep to get through. And Mickey Turner was getting closer.

Then Todd heard a sound, probably the sound he knew best in the world. Big Ben was striking eight o'clock.

Todd gazed up at the famous tower. Something was happening! It seemed to be moving, changing

shape. The great bell stopped. There was a dreadful rumbling, crashing sound and the whole tower began to fall, slowly, slowly, then with a great rush.

The top of the tower collapsed into the river, making a huge wave that swept right over the bridge.

Todd just had time to wrap his body tightly round a lamppost as the water crashed over him. And when the water went down and he could see again, the tower was just a pile of stones.

Todd looked back across the bridge, but Mickey had gone.

Todd was so exhausted he hardly noticed the rescue helicopter overhead, and the figure in the orange suit swinging down towards him.

What About Me?

by Helen Orme

Lisa's dad has been beating her mum – again. One day she finds him at home in a pool of blood. Lisa's world is suddenly turned upside-down: she has to get away. But where can she go? How will she survive?

No Good

by Helen Orme

Marie has fallen out with her parents and left home. She's moved in with her boyfriend, Jay. But her friends have heard some bad things about Jay. Can they protect Marie before things get out of hand?